OLYMPIA SOUTH
103 NE FIFTH ST.
ATLANTA, IL 61723-9712
(217) 648-2302
(217) 648-5248 (FAX)

INSIDE MLB

MINNESOTA
TWINS

BY DAVID J. CLARKE

SportsZone

An Imprint of Abdo Publishing
abdobooks.com

abdobooks.com

Published by Abdo Publishing, a division of ABDO, PO Box 398166, Minneapolis, Minnesota 55439. Copyright © 2023 by Abdo Consulting Group, Inc. International copyrights reserved in all countries. No part of this book may be reproduced in any form without written permission from the publisher. SportsZone™ is a trademark and logo of Abdo Publishing.

Printed in the United States of America, North Mankato, Minnesota.
102022
012023

THIS BOOK CONTAINS RECYCLED MATERIALS

Cover Photo: Jim McIsaac/Getty Images Sports/Getty Images
Interior Photo: Brace Hemmelgarn/Minnesota Twins/Getty Images Sport/Getty Images, 4, 32, 40; Harrison Barden/MLB/Getty Images, 6; George Rinhart/Corbis/Getty Images, 9; Bettmann/Getty Images, 10, 27; Focus on Sport/Getty Images, 12, 15, 19; William J. Smith/AP Images, 16; Mitchell Layton/Getty Images Sports/Getty Images, 20; Ron Vesely/MLB/Getty Images Sport/Getty Images, 22; Focus on Sport/Getty Images Sport/Getty Images, 25; Jim Mone/AP Images, 29; Rick Stewart/Getty Images Sport/Getty Images, 31; Dave Kaup/Getty Images Sport/Getty Images, 35; Ron Vesely/MLB/Getty Images, 37; Bruce Kluckhohn/MLB/Getty Images, 38

Editor: Steph Giedd
Series Designer: Becky Daum

Library of Congress Control Number: 2022940491

Publisher's Cataloging-in-Publication Data

Names: Clarke, David J., author.
Title: Minnesota Twins / by David J. Clarke
Description: Minneapolis, Minnesota: Abdo Publishing, 2023 | Series: Inside MLB | Includes online resources and index.
Identifiers: ISBN 9781098290245 (lib. bdg.) | ISBN 9781098275440 (ebook)
Subjects: LCSH: Minnesota Twins (Baseball team)--Juvenile literature. | Baseball teams--Juvenile literature. | Professional sports--Juvenile literature. | Sports franchises--Juvenile literature. | Major League Baseball (Organization)--Juvenile literature.
Classification: DDC 796.35764--dc23

TABLE OF CONTENTS

CHAPTER 1
SENATORS SENDOFF 4

CHAPTER 2
MEMORIES AT THE MET 12

CHAPTER 3
TWINS WIN 22

CHAPTER 4
TWINS REBORN 32

TIMELINE 42
TEAM FACTS 44
TEAM TRIVIA 45
GLOSSARY 46
MORE INFORMATION 47
ONLINE RESOURCES 47
INDEX 48
ABOUT THE AUTHOR 48

CHAPTER 1

SENATORS SENDOFF

Minnesota Twins center fielder Byron Buxton rocked in his batting stance as he awaited the 2–2 pitch. It was September 5, 2020. In the bottom of the ninth inning, the Twins had rallied to tie the Detroit Tigers 3–3. Now with two outs and runners on second and third, Buxton just needed a base hit to be a hero.

The Twins were locked in a tight race for the American League (AL) Central Division with the Chicago White Sox. With the season shortened to 60 games due to the COVID-19 pandemic, every night was crucial for playoff contenders.

Detroit reliever José Cisnero rocked and fired. The right-handed-hitting Buxton eyed the pitch. As the ball swerved low

Byron Buxton has developed into one of the sport's top hitters since making his major league debut in 2015.

Buxton sprints toward first base for a walk-off single to beat the Detroit Tigers on September 5, 2020.

and away from him, the Twins star lunged and pulled the ball off the end of his bat toward the left side of the infield. Then he took off.

Few players in baseball history have been faster than Buxton. As he sprinted full speed for first, Tigers shortstop Willi Castro charged the ball. It was an easy play against most runners. But with Buxton flying, Castro had to hurry.

Buxton's helmet flew off as he chugged toward the base. Castro's throw arrived a split second too late. Twins designated hitter Nelson Cruz trotted home with the winning run. The entire incredible play was over in less than four seconds.

Three weeks later, the Twins won the Central Division by one game over the White Sox. They were headed back to the postseason. And they had Buxton's fast feet to thank for it.

FROM WASHINGTON TO THE WEST

The Twins arrived in Minnesota in 1961. But the franchise started 60 years earlier. And it started more than 1,200 miles (1,930 kilometers) away in Washington, DC.

In the late 1890s, the only major baseball league in the United States was the National League (NL). But a new league, the Western League, started playing in the mid-1890s. By 1901 it was ready to challenge the NL at the top of the sport. The Western League renamed itself the American League. The Washington Senators were one of its original teams.

While the Senators had a spot in the new league, they were far from competitive. The team was 61–72 in the AL's first season. From there the Senators only got worse, and not just in the standings. After a decade of

BY GEORGE

In 1799 General Henry Lee gave a speech at President George Washington's funeral. He was quoted as saying Washington was "first in war, first in peace, and first in the hearts of his countrymen." After the Senators' early struggles on the field, sportswriter Charley Dryden reworked Lee's poem to make fun of the team. He famously wrote that Washington was "first in war, first in peace, and last in the American League."

losing, the Senators' rickety wooden ballpark, American League Park, burned down just before the 1911 season began.

That season the Senators moved into a new concrete ballpark. Starting in 1912, they also had a new manager. Clark Griffith had already enjoyed a long, successful career as a player and manager before he got to Washington. His arrival turned the Senators around. In 1912 Washington won 91 games. It was the team's first winning record. By the time Griffith stopped managing in 1920, he had added four more winning seasons. The only thing he didn't deliver was postseason baseball. The AL was highly competitive in the 1910s, led by teams such as the Boston Red Sox and Philadelphia Athletics. And with just one AL postseason berth each season, Griffith's Nationals routinely came up just short.

Griffith was no longer the team manager in 1921. Now he was the Senators' owner, having bought the club a year before. Under his leadership, Washington finally reached the postseason.

A GOOD YEAR

Throughout most of their early history, the Senators boasted one of baseball's best pitchers. Walter "Big Train" Johnson joined Washington in 1907, when he was discovered on a minor league team in Idaho. The lanky right-hander threw harder than anyone in the game at the time. And he racked up strikeouts for both good and bad Washington teams.

The 1924 season was one of the good years. At 36 years old, Johnson was still the ace of the pitching staff. But Washington also had a high-powered offense led by outfielders Sam Rice and Goose Goslin, as well as second baseman and team manager Bucky Harris.

Even though they finished 92–62, the Senators were big underdogs in the World Series against the New York Giants. But Washington prevailed in seven games. The Senators rallied late in Game 7 to force extra innings. Then Johnson came in to shut New York down. Washington finally won in the 12th on a walk-off double.

Washington Senators pitcher Walter "Big Train" Johnson threw a record 110 shutouts in his career.

Senators shortstop Joe Cronin became a player/manager in 1933.

GO WEST

The Senators made it back to the World Series a year later. But any chance at a repeat was lost when they blew a 3–1 series lead against the Pittsburgh Pirates. Then Johnson let a 7–6 lead slip away in the eighth inning of Game 7. The Pirates won 9–7.

Johnson retired after the 1927 season and managed a minor league team in 1928. A year later, he became the Senators' manager. He continued to build the program until 1933, when Joe Cronin took over as player/manager. He led the Senators back to the World Series in 1933, only to lose in five games against the Giants. For the rest of the team's 27 years in Washington, the Senators put together only four winning seasons.

By the late 1950s, the landscape of baseball was changing. Teams were moving away from eastern cities and heading west. Soon the Senators, now owned by Griffith's nephew Calvin, joined the rush. As a new decade dawned, the Senators were on the lookout for a new home.

BY ANY OTHER NAME

Though the team was known as the Washington "Senators" by baseball fans, the official nickname was not Senators for most of the team's history. The Senators officially changed their nickname to Nationals in 1905. It stayed that way until 1956. Since most fans still called them the Senators, Washington officially changed the name back five years before leaving town.

CHAPTER 2

MEMORIES AT THE MET

The Senators struggled throughout the 1950s. And with poor records, they drew few fans. Tired of losing money, owner Calvin Griffith started looking for a new home. After trying several locations, including both San Francisco and Los Angeles, Griffith eventually made a deal to move the team to Minnesota after the 1960 season.

With the move, the team needed a new name. Griffith settled on the Twins after the Twin Cities of Minneapolis and St. Paul. He was concerned that if the team's name had either Minneapolis or St. Paul in it, fans from the other city wouldn't come to games. He originally wanted to call them the Twin

Twins slugger Harmon Killebrew bats at Metropolitan Stadium in Bloomington, Minnesota.

Cities Twins. But Major League Baseball (MLB) rejected the name, so the team was known as the Minnesota Twins.

Despite being named after both of Minnesota's large cities, the Twins did not play in either Minneapolis or St. Paul. Their ballpark, Metropolitan Stadium, was in the Minneapolis suburb of Bloomington.

KILLER AND TONY O.

The team arrived in Minnesota with several great hitters already on the roster. Outfielder Bob Allison and catcher Earl Battey were consistent home run threats. As the 1960s rolled on, the Twins added more power from center fielder Jimmie Hall.

However, the main Minnesota slugger was Harmon Killebrew. The 6-foot, 195-pound Killebrew led the majors in home runs five times during the 1960s while playing first base, third base, and left field for the Twins. An upbringing hauling heavy milk cans on his family's Idaho farm had made Killebrew naturally strong. And his ability to hammer a baseball earned him the nickname "Killer."

The Twins' other big-hitting star came from a foreign baseball hotbed. Outfielder Tony Oliva left Cuba to play in the minor leagues in 1961. He later joined the Twins late in the 1962 season. By 1964 "Tony O." was an elite hitter. As a rookie, his

.323 average led the AL. He did it again in 1965 by hitting .321. No MLB player had ever been a batting champion his first two seasons before Oliva.

SUMMER OF '65

Minnesota surged to the AL pennant in 1965. Even though Killebrew was injured and missed nearly 50 games, the Twins still led the AL in runs. That offense carried the team to a 102–60 record under manager Sam Mele.

In the franchise's first World Series since 1933, the Twins faced the Los Angeles Dodgers. While the Twins were a slugging team, the Dodgers relied mostly on pitching. Hall of Famers Don Drysdale and Sandy Koufax led the Los Angeles staff. However, the Twins beat both in winning the first two games at Metropolitan Stadium.

Tony Oliva takes off toward first base after getting a hit for the Twins.

Pitcher Jim "Mudcat" Grant gave up only one hit in a 5–0 victory against the Washington Senators in a 1965 matchup.

Then Minnesota's bats went quiet over the next three games in Los Angeles. The Twins scored only two total runs during that time. Koufax struck out 10 Minnesota batters in the fifth game and allowed only two hits.

In a desperation Game 6, the Twins bounced back. Allison hit a two-run home run in the fourth inning to give Minnesota the lead. Then Jim "Mudcat" Grant did the rest. The Twins pitcher went the distance, allowing only six hits in a 5–1 complete game win.

In a series of great pitching performances, nothing topped Koufax in Game 7. All seven games of the series were played in a span of nine days. That meant that from the time Koufax finished his shutout in Game 5, he had only two days off before Game 7. But he pitched a masterpiece, shutting out the Twins on only three hits. Minnesota's first trip to the World Series had come up empty.

CHASING WILLIAMS

In 1969 MLB expanded its playoffs to include two teams from each league. The Twins were the first winners of the AL's new Western Division that year. They won it again in 1970. Despite that, they could not get past the dominant Baltimore Orioles either year in the newly created AL Championship Series (ALCS).

TOVAR DOES IT ALL

In a 1968 game against the Oakland Athletics, the Twins' Cesar Tovar played all nine positions. He pitched a shutout first inning. Then he moved to catcher in the second inning. After that he spent the next seven innings playing each infield and outfield spot. He became just the second MLB player ever to accomplish the feat. On top of his fielding adventures, Tovar went 1-for-3 at the plate and scored the first run of a 2–1 Twins victory.

Even worse, the Twins were getting old. Killebrew, while still one of the game's best sluggers, turned 34 in 1970. Allison was 35. Oliva was 31. Ace pitchers Jim Kaat and Jim Perry were also over 30. As those players aged even further, the Twins couldn't keep pace in the AL.

The 1970s brought even bigger changes to MLB. Until then owners had full control over player contracts. They decided every year who to keep and who to cut. That changed in 1976, when free agency was introduced. Owners hated it, and few despised it more than Griffith.

Griffith had always been tight with money. Now that players had more power to negotiate contracts, he fought them for every dollar. During the 1970s, that meant several tough negotiations with the Twins' biggest star, infielder Rod Carew.

While the Twins struggled in the standings during the decade, Carew was a one-man show. The left-handed hitter was consistently one of the best in baseball. He joined the Twins as a second baseman in 1967. Two years later, he won his first batting title. That was just a warm-up. Starting in 1972, Carew led the AL in hitting in six of the next seven years.

Carew's best season came in 1977. That June he hit an amazing .487. No player had finished a season with a .400 batting average since the great Ted Williams in 1941. Baseball fans wondered if Carew could do it. On July 1 his batting average reached .411. Even Williams offered his support. But Carew's average dipped back below .400 for good on July 11. Fans watched and waited all summer for the next hot streak to bring his number back up. It never came, but Carew still finished the season at .388. That was the best average MLB had seen in 20 years.

THE TWINS GO INDOORS

In September 1978, Griffith gave a speech to a Lions Club in southern Minnesota. In it he made several racist statements. He also boasted that he was paying Carew much less than the star player was worth. When a Minneapolis newspaper broke the story about the speech, fans

Twins first baseman Rod Carew led the majors in 1977 with a .388 batting average.

The Metrodome was not ideal for baseball games with its springy artificial turf, low roof, and mediocre sightlines.

were outraged. Many suggested that Griffith sell the team his family had owned since 1920.

Carew was also disgusted. He called Griffith a bigot and compared playing for him to toiling on a slave plantation. The team's best player refused to ever play for Minnesota again. He was traded to the California Angels later that winter.

Griffith did not sell the team right away. Instead, he moved them to a new stadium in 1982. After 21 years playing outdoors, the Twins moved into the Hubert H. Humphrey Metrodome in downtown Minneapolis.

The Metrodome was one of baseball's strangest stadiums. Baseballs bounced like rubber balls on the springy artificial turf. It had an inflatable roof that was a dirty shade of white. Balls that went up were nearly invisible. While Twins outfielders got used to tracking fly balls very closely, visitors often lost them completely. The roof was also low enough that balls would sometimes hit it, changing their path on the way down.

The stadium was also incredibly loud. During a Twins playoff run, stadium staff installed a decibel meter to read the level of noise. The loudest reading checked in at 125 decibels. That's slightly lower than a jet taking off.

WHAT GOES UP

Among the Metrodome's other strange characteristics were several holes in the roof. Twice during MLB games, balls went up and through one of them and never came down. Following the official park ground rules, the batters were awarded doubles.

However, few fans showed up to watch the Twins during their first two years indoors. Griffith was almost ready to move the team again, this time to Tampa, Florida. Instead, he finally decided to sell. Banker Carl Pohlad bought the Twins in 1984. That year, a team filled with young, promising players finished 81–81. Twins fans were hopeful that a return to greatness was right around the corner.

CHAPTER 3

TWINS WIN

On May 8, 1984, Kirby Puckett made his Twins debut. The 5-foot-8-inch, 178-pound center fielder went 4-for-5 in his first game, and a Minnesota icon was born.

Puckett was short and stocky, but he could do it all on a baseball field. At the plate, he seemingly swung at everything, and he usually made contact. In the field, he gave a full effort to make highlight plays. With Puckett the Twins had a star they could build around for years to come. He was hardly the only young player to arrive in the early 1980s, though.

Burly first baseman Kent Hrbek had grown up just minutes from Metropolitan Stadium as a kid. He debuted for the Twins late in the 1981 season. Hard-nosed third baseman Gary Gaetti

Kirby Puckett sprints to the next base in a 1988 game against the Milwaukee Brewers. That season he led the majors in at-bats (657), hits (234), and total bases (358).

also played a few games in 1981. After becoming a starter the next season, he rarely took a day off. Meanwhile, left-handed pitcher Frank Viola made his major league debut in 1982. He grew into an ace over the next few years. Bringing them all together was Tom Kelly, who came aboard as manager late in the 1986 season.

That year the Twins won 71 games and finished sixth in the AL West. One year later, Minnesota won the division title. Puckett, Gaetti, Hrbek, and right fielder Tom Brunansky supplied the power. Viola was joined in the rotation by 36-year-old Bert Blyleven. The right-hander returned to the Twins in 1985 after playing his early years in Minnesota. His best seasons were behind him, but he still featured one of baseball's top curveballs.

The 1987 Twins were far from perfect. They gave up more runs than they scored. Aside from Viola and Blyleven, few pitchers stood out. Minnesota was also terrible on the road, winning only 29 of 81 games. But the Twins finished 56–25 at the Metrodome.

Luckily for the Twins, they got to open the ALCS at home. MLB rules at the time alternated home field advantage every year. In 1987 it was the West Division's turn. The Twins rode that advantage to a 4–1 series win over the heavily favored Detroit Tigers.

Kent Hrbek played his entire 14-year career in Minnesota.

World Series home field advantage was also traded between leagues every year. Once again the Twins got lucky. The NL champion St. Louis Cardinals had a much better record than Minnesota's mark of 85–77, but four World Series games were scheduled for the Metrodome. Game 1 would be the first-ever indoor World Series game.

VIOLA'S SWEET MUSIC

The Twins blitzed St. Louis in the first two games. Left fielder Dan Gladden's fourth-inning grand slam backed Viola in a 10–1 Game 1 win. Then Blyleven pitched an 8–4 victory in Game 2.

However, just as in 1965, the Twins were swept in the NL park. That set up another desperation Game 6. Back in the Metrodome and needing a win to stay alive, the Twins turned on the offense again. Minnesota led 6–5 in the bottom of the sixth inning when Hrbek stepped up to the plate with the bases loaded. The hometown hero belted a grand slam to center field to break the game open in an 11–6 win.

There had never been a World Series in which the home team had won all seven games. To break that trend in Game 7, the Twins turned to Viola, whose nickname was "Sweet Music." St. Louis built a 2–0 lead in the second inning before the Minnesota ace settled down. He lasted eight innings while the Twins fought back. They tied the game in the fifth inning and then took the lead in the sixth. Shortstop Greg Gagne, known mostly for defense, singled home Brunansky for a 3–2 edge.

In the ninth inning, Twins closer Jeff Reardon came on to hold a 4–2 lead. Cardinals outfielder Willie McGee bounced a two-out grounder to Gaetti at third base. He fired across to Hrbek for the championship-clinching out and Minnesota's first World Series title.

WORST TO FIRST

By 1990 the Twins had dropped to last place. When the 1991 season opened, only seven players remained from the

Twins player Roy Smalley, *top*, jumps on first baseman Kent Hrbek (14) in celebration of their World Series victory over the St. Louis Cardinals.

1987 team. But that core included Hrbek, Puckett, Gladden, and Gagne. They were joined by rookie second baseman Chuck Knoblauch, who went on to win the AL Rookie of the Year Award.

The 1991 team also had two young, promising starting pitchers in Kevin Tapani and Scott Erickson. To give them help, the Twins signed another local Minnesotan. Jack Morris had grown up in St. Paul, just miles from where the Metrodome now stood. After an excellent career with the Tigers, he came home with a reputation as a tough, big-game pitcher.

Even with the additions, things still didn't look good in June. The Twins entered the month just 23–25. But a 15-game winning streak that month surged Minnesota ahead in the race. The Twins stayed in first for the rest of the year.

The worst-to-first Twins then rocked the Toronto Blue Jays 4–1 in the ALCS to set up an improbable World Series. The NL champions were the Atlanta Braves, who had also finished last in their league in 1990. No team had ever jumped from last place to World Series champion in one season. Now it was a guarantee, no matter who won.

What followed was one of the most nail-biting World Series ever played. Three of the first five games were decided by one run. The home team won them all, meaning the Twins returned to the Metrodome for Game 6 down 3–2.

JUMP ON MY BACK

Puckett had been quiet in the Series. He was just 3-for-18 with one run batted in (RBI) through five games. There was no denting his confidence, however. Before Game 6, he told his teammates, "Jump on my back. I'll carry you."

Puckett backed up his claim in the first inning with an RBI triple. In the third inning, he got his glove in on the act. With the Twins up 2–0, Atlanta third baseman Terry Pendleton was on first with one out. Two batters later, center fielder Ron Gant

Puckett celebrates his solo walk-off home run in Game 6 of the 1991 World Series.

crushed a ball toward the wall in left-center field. Puckett raced back and timed his jump, snagging the ball just before it hit the plexiglass extension to the outfield fence. The talented Twins center fielder was keeping his promise to his team.

Even with Puckett's heroics, the Twins struggled to shake Atlanta. As the tense game reached the bottom of the 11th inning, Puckett led off against Atlanta lefty Charlie Leibrandt. The Twins' center fielder then sent Leibrandt's 2-1 pitch over the left-field fence for a thrilling 4–3 win. As he rounded the bases to a loud cheer, Puckett pumped his fist and screamed along with the fans. On the night, he was 3-for-4 with a triple, a home run, and three RBIs. TV announcer Jack Buck concluded the walk-off win in fitting fashion by saying, "And we'll see you tomorrow night!"

PUCKETT CALLS HIS SHOT

Almost two decades after the 1991 World Series win, former hitting coach Terry Crowley revealed that Kirby Puckett predicted his dramatic Game 6 home run. As the slugger was watching Charlie Leibrandt warm up, Puckett turned to Crowley and said, "Crow, if they leave this guy in the game, it's over."

HOMETOWN HERO

The dramatic Game 6 became an instant classic. Morris and Atlanta righty John Smoltz followed it up with one of the great pitching duels in World Series history. Smoltz shut out the Twins for 7 1/3 innings before relievers took over. Morris topped him by blanking Atlanta for 10 innings.

Gladden then led off the bottom half of the 10th with a double. Four batters later, he was on third with one out and the

Jack Morris struck out eight batters while giving up just seven hits and two walks during his 10-inning shutout in Game 7 of the 1991 World Series.

bases loaded. Pinch-hitter Gene Larkin stepped into the box. Atlanta Manager Bobby Cox pulled his outfielders in close to the infield so they might have a chance to throw out Gladden at home on a short fly ball. Larkin then blasted the first pitch he saw over the left fielder's head. Gladden trotted home, where Morris was the first one to meet him at home plate. Morris was named the World Series Most Valuable Player (MVP). His 10-inning shutout is considered one of the greatest World Series pitching performances ever.

CHAPTER 4

TWINS REBORN

After winning the World Series in 1991, the Twins' fortunes dropped dramatically for the rest of the decade. Jack Morris left the team after his World Series heroics. Kent Hrbek retired in 1994. But perhaps the biggest blow came the following year. Kirby Puckett was hit in the head by a pitch late in the 1995 season, ending his year. During spring training, he announced he had developed glaucoma in his right eye. With his vision damaged, he was also forced to retire.

Even worse, baseball's finances were getting away from the Twins. While big clubs like the New York Yankees handed out huge contracts to stars, smaller markets like Minnesota struggled to keep players. Playing in the outdated Metrodome

Twins center fielder Torii Hunter prepares to bat against the Chicago White Sox at Target Field in Minneapolis, Minnesota.

didn't help. In 2000 the Twins were paying their players $16.5 million total. By contrast, the Yankees paid their roster $92.5 million. That year Minnesota finished with a losing record for the eighth year in a row.

CONTRACTION

The young, cheap Twins improved to 85–77 in 2001. But in November, MLB owners voted 28–2 to eliminate two teams. The owners wouldn't publicly reveal which two teams would be eliminated, but many understood that it would be the Twins and the Montreal Expos.

Twins fans were outraged. The team had promising young players like pitcher Brad Radke and speedy shortstop Cristian Guzman. Torii Hunter was developing into a highlight-film center fielder, just like Puckett before him.

Less than two weeks after the vote, a Minnesota judge hearing a lawsuit on the plan ruled that the Twins were too important to the community to fold. He ordered the team to keep playing in 2002. MLB backed down, and both Montreal and Minnesota played on. Then in August, the owners agreed to stop trying to eliminate any teams.

The Twins made the most of their new life. Ron Gardenhire took over for the now-retired Tom Kelly as Minnesota's manager before the season. He led an improbable playoff run.

First baseman Justin Morneau stretches to get an out against the Kansas City Royals in 2004.

Despite having the fourth-lowest payroll in MLB, the Twins won the AL Central Division by 13 1/2 games. Then they knocked off the Oakland Athletics in a five-game AL Division Series (ALDS).

While the Twins' amazing run ended in the ALCS against the Anaheim Angels, Minnesota fans knew the team would survive.

THE PIRANHAS

Minnesota followed up the 2002 season with two more AL Central titles in 2003 and 2004. But playoff success was harder to come by. The Twins met the powerhouse Yankees in the five-game ALDS each time. Both years Minnesota lost in four games.

Still, the Twins were now loaded with top stars. Slugging first baseman Justin Morneau debuted in 2003. Three years later, he was AL MVP. Hunter provided power to go with athletic center-field play.

On the mound, flamethrowing closer Joe Nathan was one of the AL's best. Radke was still a steady control pitcher. But the Twins' ace was a lefthander named Johan Santana. The Venezuelan struggled early in his career. But he mastered the change-up after going back to the minor leagues. When he came back to the Twins, he dominated hitters. Santana won Cy Young Awards in 2004 and 2006 as the best pitcher in the AL.

The Twins' pitching staff also threw to one of the game's best-ever catchers. Like Hrbek and Morris before him, Joe Mauer was a local Minnesotan. The Twins plucked him with the top pick in the 2001 draft.

By 2006 Mauer was one of the game's top hitters. Despite the defensive demands of catching, he hit .347 as the Twins finished 96–66 to win the Central Division again. Mauer's smooth swing and Morneau's power were complemented by several role players. In an era of home-run hitting, the Twins mostly succeeded by playing small ball. They were fundamentally sound, stole bases, and played great defense. Three undersized players signified this group. Shortstop Jason Bartlett, utilityman Nick Punto, and reserve outfielder Jason Tyner combined for only three home runs in 2006. But their scrappy play earned them the nickname "Piranhas" from Chicago White Sox manager Ozzie Guillen.

Neither the Twins' stars nor the Piranhas could get them over the playoff hump, however. The Twins were swept in the ALDS by the Oakland A's.

Twins catcher Joe Mauer led the AL in batting average in 2006, 2008, and 2009. In 2009 he was also voted the AL MVP.

RIGHT ON TARGET

On October 6, 2009, the Twins and Detroit Tigers held a one-game playoff at the Metrodome for the AL Central Division title. The thrilling game went into the 12th inning tied 5–5. With one out and two runners on, Minnesota designated hitter Alexi Casilla slapped a single to right field. Speedy outfielder Carlos Gomez raced home for the winning run. The Twins were headed to the playoffs for the fifth time in the decade. It was a thrilling win

This 2014 photo shows Target Field in the heart of downtown Minneapolis.

for Minnesota. However, the season ended in a familiar way: a sweep by the Yankees.

Game 3 was played at the Metrodome. The 4–1 New York win was the final baseball game ever at the indoor ballpark. The following spring, the Twins moved into Target Field, their gleaming new home in downtown Minneapolis. With the new open-air park, the Twins' future was finally fully secure.

However, the first year of Target Field ended just as the final years of the Metrodome had. Once again the Twins met the Yankees in the playoffs. And once again, New York won all three games.

The Twins' lineup was also changing. By 2010 Radke had retired. Hunter left as a free agent, and Santana had been traded. Halfway through the 2010 season, Morneau suffered a concussion that ruined his career.

Mauer was still going strong, having been named AL MVP in 2009. But over the next five years, the demands of catching led to several injuries, and he was moved to first base in 2014. As Mauer struggled, so did the Twins. They missed the playoffs for six straight years starting in 2011.

TWINS TURNAROUND

The Twins have had several impressive season-to-season turnarounds in their history, but the one in 2017 was particularly notable. In 2016 the Twins finished 59–103. A year later, they improved to 85–77. Though they lost the AL wild-card game to the New York Yankees, Minnesota became the first MLB club to reach the playoffs one year after losing 100 games.

BOMBA SQUAD

Starting in the late 1990s, home runs increased throughout baseball. Even the successful Twins teams of the 2000s were among the least powerful in the league. But in the 2010s, that started to change. Led by sluggers such as All-Star second baseman Brian Dozier, third baseman Miguel Sanó, and outfielders Max Kepler, Eddie Rosario, and Byron Buxton, in 2017 the Twins hit 200 home runs for the first time in 52 years.

Luis Arraez earned his first All-Star team appearance in his fourth season with the Twins in 2022.

A year later, that power surge boosted Minnesota back to the playoffs. However, they lost the AL wild-card playoff to the Yankees.

During the 2019 season, MLB teams slugged homers at record pace. The Twins entered their game against the Tigers on August 31 with 262 dingers, five shy of the Yankees' one-year-old record of 267. That day Minnesota hit six total.

Designated hitter Nelson Cruz led the team with 41, and 10 other players hit double figures. But the Twins had to hold off the Yankees to keep the record at season's end. On the last day of the year, catcher Jason Castro's solo shot in the fifth inning was the team's 307th of the year. That edged the Yankees, who finished with 306.

Many of Minnesota's stars grew up as native Spanish speakers. Early in the year, Rosario, who was from Puerto Rico, was quoted as saying, "I hit a *bomba*," using the Spanish word for "bomb." The team became known as "the Bomba Squad."

All those home runs didn't help the Twins in the playoffs. Incredibly, the Twins lost to the Yankees in a three-game ALDS sweep again.

THE STREAK

The Bomba Squad returned to the playoffs in 2020. Weary Twins fans were relieved not to see the Yankees in the other dugout. Instead, Minnesota faced the Houston Astros. It didn't matter. The Astros won the best-of-three AL wild-card series 2–0. The Twins failed to homer and scored only a single run in each game. The Game 1 loss was Minnesota's 17th straight playoff defeat. That broke the record for major American professional teams in all sports.

Entering the 2022 season, the Twins focused their lineup around Buxton. With his blinding speed, he made a habit of impossible catches in center field and flying around the bases. And the addition of Luis Arraez in 2019 added another big bat to the lineup. With the young rising hitters such as Buxton and Arraez, and a beautiful ballpark to call home, the Twins had their fans feeling optimistic about the team's future.

TIMELINE

1901
The Washington Senators join the new American League as one of its charter members.

1920
Former MLB player and manager Clark Griffith purchases the Senators.

1924
Led by Hall of Fame pitcher Walter Johnson, the Senators defeat the New York Giants 4–3 to win the franchise's first World Series.

1933
The Senators reach the World Series but lose to the Giants. It is the team's last World Series appearance while playing in Washington, DC.

1955
Clark Griffith's nephew Calvin takes over as principal owner of the team.

1961
Griffith moves the Senators to Minnesota and renames them the Twins.

1965
The Twins reach the World Series but lose in seven games to the Los Angeles Dodgers.

1977
Minnesota second baseman Rod Carew nearly hits .400 for the season but settles to an average of .388 at the end of the year.

1982
The Twins move indoors to play at the Hubert H. Humphrey Metrodome.

1984
Calvin Griffith sells the Twins to Carl Pohlad.

1987
The Twins win their first World Series since moving to Minnesota, topping the St. Louis Cardinals 4–3.

1991
Minnesota becomes the first team to win the World Series after finishing in last place the year before. They beat the Atlanta Braves in a thrilling seven-game series.

2001
MLB votes 28–2 to contract two teams, believed to be the Twins and the Montreal Expos. However, both teams continue playing after a Minnesota judge orders the Twins to fulfill their Metrodome lease.

2002
The Twins surprise many by winning the AL Central. They win the division in 2003 and 2004 as well.

2010
The Twins open their new ballpark, Target Field, in downtown Minneapolis.

2019
Minnesota's "Bomba Squad" sets a new MLB record by hitting 307 home runs in a season.

2020
The Twins lose the AL wild-card series 2–0 to the Houston Astros, extending Minnesota's record of playoff-game losses to 18.

TEAM FACTS

FRANCHISE HISTORY
Washington Senators (1901–60)
Minnesota Twins (1961–)

WORLD SERIES CHAMPIONSHIPS
1924, 1987, 1991

KEY PLAYERS
Bob Allison (1958–70)
Bert Blyleven (1970–76, 1985–88)
Byron Buxton (2015–)
Rod Carew (1967–78)
Goose Goslin (1921–30, 1933, 1938)
Kent Hrbek (1981–94)
Torii Hunter (1997–07, 2015)
Walter Johnson (1907–27)
Jim Kaat (1959–73)
Harmon Killebrew (1954–74)
Joe Mauer (2004–18)
Justin Morneau (2003–13)
Tony Oliva (1962–76)
Kirby Puckett (1984–95)
Brad Radke (1995–06)
Sam Rice (1915–33)
Johan Santana (2000–07)
Frank Viola (1982–89)

KEY MANAGERS
Ron Gardenhire (2002–14)
Bucky Harris (1924–28, 1935–42, 1950–54)
Tom Kelly (1986–2001)

HOME STADIUMS
American League Park (1901–03)
American League Park II (1904–11)
  Also known as:
  National Park (1904–05)
Griffith Stadium (1911–60)
  Also known as:
  National Park (1911–20)
Metropolitan Stadium (1961–81)
Hubert H. Humphrey Metrodome (1982–2009)
Target Field (2010–)

TEAM TRIVIA

PRESIDENTIAL PITCH

The Senators began the tradition of presidents throwing out the first pitch on Opening Day in 1910, when William Howard Taft did it before a Senators opener against the Philadelphia Athletics.

DOUBLE TRIPLE

The Twins became the first team to turn two triple plays in the same game when they did so on July 17, 1990, against the Boston Red Sox. Both plays were turned by third baseman Gary Gaetti, second baseman Al Newman, and first baseman Kent Hrbek.

THE MALL

The Mall of America sits on the site of the old Metropolitan Stadium. The mall still features a bronze plaque where the original home plate stood and a seat on a wall 522 feet away, where Harmon Killebrew hit the longest home run in stadium history.

MINOR LEAGUE MINNESOTA

Prior to the Twins, both Minneapolis and St. Paul were home to minor league teams. The Minneapolis Millers were a farm team for both the Boston Red Sox and New York Giants. The Saints were affiliated with the Chicago White Sox and Brooklyn/Los Angeles Dodgers. Both teams folded in 1960, but a new version of the Saints returned in 1993. In 2021 the Saints became the Twins' new Triple A affiliate.

GLOSSARY

ace
A team's best starting pitcher.

bigot
A person who treats behaves badly toward members of other groups, such as people of another race or ethnicity.

contraction
A legal process for removing teams from an existing sports league.

draft
A system that allows teams to acquire new players coming into a league.

franchise
A sports organization, including the top-level team and all minor league affiliates.

free agent
A player whose rights are not owned by any team.

ground rules
Rules that are specific to a stadium or ballpark.

pennant
Another name for a league championship; in MLB, refers to winning either the American or National League.

racist
Discriminating against other people based only on their race.

rookie
A professional athlete in his or her first year of competition.

utilityman
A member of a baseball team who plays various positions in the absence of regular players.

walk-off
Any victory in which the home team scores the winning run in the bottom of the final inning.

MORE INFORMATION

BOOKS

Flynn, Brendan. *The MLB Encyclopedia*. Minneapolis, MN: Abdo Publishing, 2022.

Hewson, Anthony K. *GOATs of Baseball*. Minneapolis, MN: Abdo Publishing, 2022.

Mitchell, Bo. *Ultimate MLB Road Trip*. Minneapolis, MN: Abdo Publishing, 2019.

ONLINE RESOURCES

To learn more about the Minnesota Twins, please visit **abdobooklinks.com** or scan this QR code. These links are routinely monitored and updated to provide the most current information available.

INDEX

Allison, Bob, 14, 16, 18

Bartlett, Jason, 36
Battey, Earl, 14
Blyleven, Bert, 24–25
Brunansky, Tom, 24, 26
Buxton, Byron, 5–7, 39, 41

Carew, Rod, 18–20
Casilla, Alexi, 37
Castro, Jason, 40
Cronin, Joe, 11
Crowley, Terry, 30
Cruz, Nelson, 6, 40

Dozier, Brian, 39

Erickson, Scott, 27

Gaetti, Gary, 23–24, 26
Gagne, Greg, 26–27
Gardenhire, Ron, 34
Gladden, Dan, 25, 27, 30–31
Gomez, Carlos, 37
Goslin, Goose, 9
Grant, Jim, 16
Griffith, Calvin, 11, 13, 18–21
Griffith, Clark, 8, 11
Guzman, Cristian, 34

Harris, Bucky, 9
Hrbek, Kent, 23–24, 26–27, 33, 36
Hunter, Torii, 34, 36, 39

Johnson, Walter, 8–9, 11

Kaat, Jim, 18
Kelly, Tom, 24, 34
Kepler, Max, 39
Killebrew, Harmon, 14–15, 18
Knoblauch, Chuck, 27

Larkin, Gene, 30–31

Mauer, Joe, 36, 39
Morneau, Justin, 36, 39
Morris, Jack, 27, 30–31, 33, 36

Nathan, Joe, 36

Oliva, Tony, 14–15, 18

Perry, Jim, 18
Pohlad, Carl, 21
Puckett, Kirby, 23–24, 27–30, 33–34
Punto, Nick, 36

Radke, Brad, 34, 36, 39
Reardon, Jeff, 26
Rice, Sam, 9
Rosario, Eddie, 39, 41

Sanó, Miguel, 39
Santana, Johan, 36, 39

Tapani, Kevin, 27
Tovar, Cesar, 17
Tyner, Jason, 37

Viola, Frank, 24–26

Williams, Ted, 18–19

ABOUT THE AUTHOR

David J. Clarke is a freelance writer. Originally from Helena, Montana, he now lives in Savannah, Georgia, with his golden retriever, Gus.